Lighting the Night

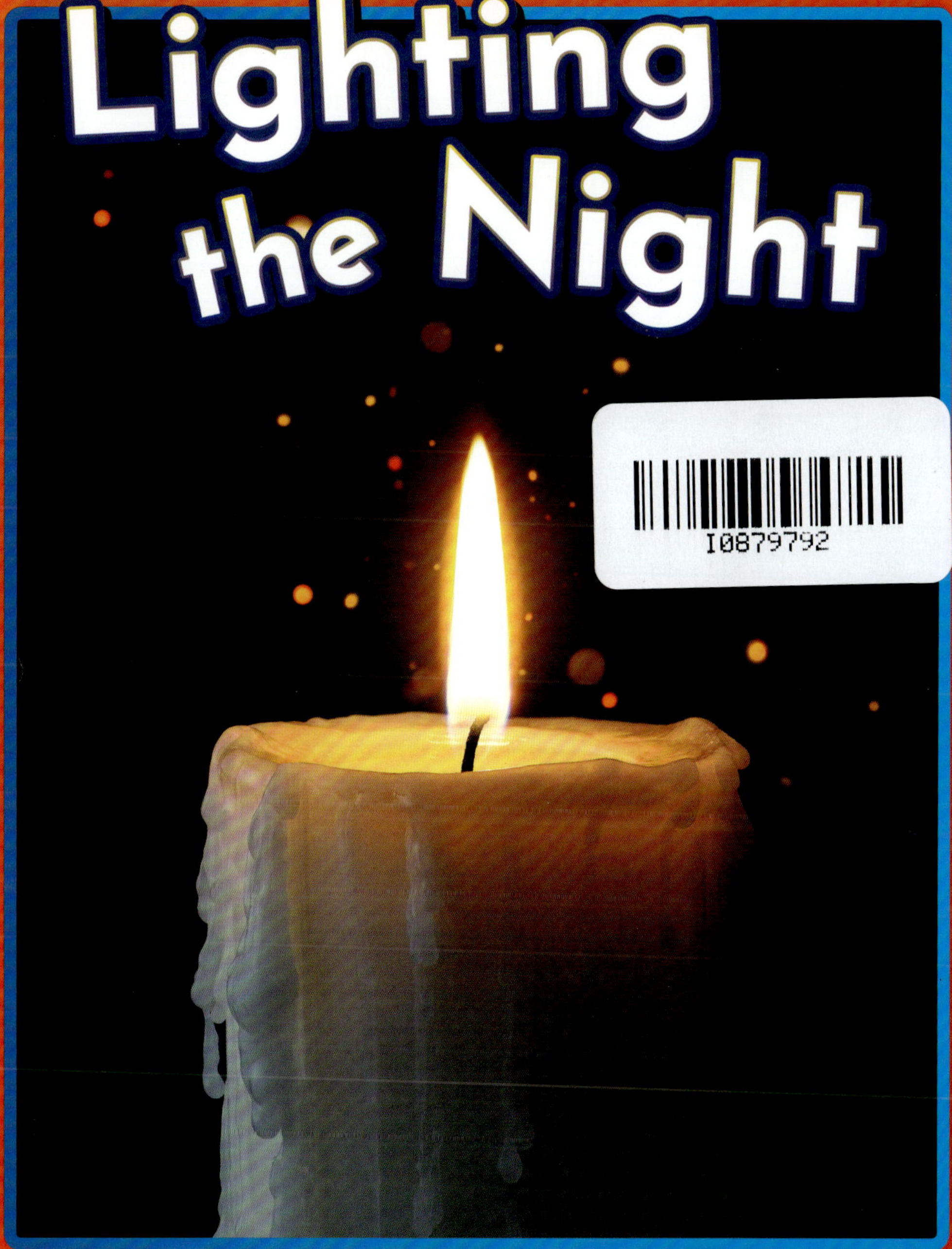

Nellie Wilder

Smithsonian

light by fire

light by candle

light by oil lamp

light by gas lamp

light by light bulb

light by flashlight

light by headlamp

light the night

STEAM CHALLENGE

The Problem

You need to add light to a dollhouse. You only have one flashlight.

The Goals

- Use a cardboard box as the dollhouse room.
- Make a small lamp with a shade.
- The lamp should light up the area that you want.

1 Research and Brainstorm

Learn about light.

2 Design and Build

Draw your plan. Build your lamp and shade!

3 Test and Improve

Test the lamp and shade. Then, try to make it better.

4 Reflect and Share

What did you learn?

Consultants

Amy Zoque
STEM Coordinator and Instructional Coach
Vineyard STEM School
Ontario Montclair District

Siobhan Tangney
Marblehead Elementary
Capistrano Unified School District

Publishing Credits

Rachelle Cracchiolo, M.S.Ed., *Publisher*
Conni Medina, M.A.Ed., *Editor in Chief*
Diana Kenney, M.A.Ed., NBCT, *Series Developer*
Emily R. Smith, M.A.Ed., *Content Director*
Véronique Bos, *Creative Director*
Robin Erickson, *Art Director*
Stephanie Bernard, *Associate Editor*
Mindy Duits, *Senior Graphic Designer*
Smithsonian Science Education Center

Image Credits: all images from Shutterstock and/or iStock.

Library of Congress Cataloging-in-Publication Data

Names: Wilder, Nellie, author.
Title: Lighting the night / Nellie Wilder.
Description: Huntington Beach, CA : Teacher Created Materials, [2020] | "Smithsonian Institution"--Copyright statement. | Includes index. | Audience: Age 5. | Audience: K to grade 3. |
Identifiers: LCCN 2018055258 (print) | LCCN 2019009545 (ebook) | ISBN 9781425859800 (eBook) | ISBN 9781493866359 | ISBN 9781493866359- (pbk.) |
ISBN 1493866354(pbk.)
Subjects: LCSH: Light sources--Juvenile literature. | Light and darkness--Juvenile literature. | Light--Juvenile literature.
Classification: LCC QC360 (ebook) | LCC QC360 .W54 2020 (print) | DDC 535--dc23
LC record available at https://lccn.loc.gov/2018055258

Smithsonian

Teacher Created Materials
5301 Oceanus Drive
Huntington Beach, CA 92649-1030
www.tcmpub.com
ISBN 978-1-4938-6635-9

Printed in China WAI002